Contents

COLOUR FIRST READER books are perfect for beginner readers. All the text inside this Colour First Reader book has been checked and approved by a reading specialist, so it is the ideal size, length and level for children learning to read.

Series Reading Consultant: Prue Goodwin
Honorary Fellow of the University of Reading

Chapter One

Jessica's granny wasn't like
other grannies. She never wore
a shawl or a flowery dress or
sensible shoes to help bad feet.
In fact, the day Jessica went to
see Granny about her tooth,

Granny was wearing a
cowboy outfit. Granny
was in her kitchen but
she wasn't doing granny
things like knitting or
cooking. She was dancing.
It was a Tuesday and Granny
went line dancing on Tuesdays.

"Granny," said Jessica, a bit
excited, "it's happened!"

"That's wonderful," exclaimed
Granny. Then she leant forward
and whispered, "What has?"

Jessica smiled at her. Right in the middle of her mouth was a large gap.

"My tooth has come out!"

Jessica felt in her pocket and pulled out a small piece of tissue paper. Inside was a small but perfect white tooth, which, that morning, had been helping Jessica to eat an apple.

"That's marvellous," declared Granny, doing a short tap dance in her cowboy boots.

"I think this calls for champagne, don't you?"

Jessica nodded. She knew it wasn't real champagne but they had the drink in champagne glasses anyway.

"Are you going to leave it under your pillow?" Granny asked, while she poured the drinks.

Jessica nodded. "Oh, yes. My friend Katie got a pound for her tooth."

"Splendid," beamed Granny, "at last I can tell you."

"Tell me what?" asked Jessica.

Granny put the drinks on the kitchen table and sat down.

"About the troublesome tooth fairy.

"I promised to keep it a secret
till I had a grandchild of my
own who lost a tooth." Granny
settled down to her story.

"It happened to me when I
was your age. I had a
troublesome tooth fairy."

"Troublesome? What do you
mean?" asked Jessica, wide-eyed
and toothless.

"Well, it was all rather surprising. I must have been about six, maybe seven.

My tooth came out after a rather nasty fall from an apple tree. To be honest, I was lucky to survive at all."

13

"Because of the fall?"

"No. Because of the tooth fairy. Oh, she was hopeless. A real first-timer." Granny took a sip of pink champagne before she carried on.

"It was the first tooth I had lost. At bedtime my mother wrapped it in a lace handkerchief and placed it under my pillow.

"I remember I was so excited that I lay watching my pillow by the light of the moon. But I must have fallen asleep because, the next thing I knew, the clock in the hall was striking four in the morning. I opened my eyes and saw a shadow at the window. A small, mysterious shadow . . ."

Chapter Two

It was the tooth fairy, but it was not the efficient leave-you-your-money-and-take-the-tooth fairy that I was expecting. No, this was a hopeless tooth fairy. A troublesome, trainee tooth fairy.

She was about fifteen centimetres tall and dressed in purple and silver. She looked lovely, but I didn't realize that it was because her tooth fairy outfit was brand-new. You see, she had never been to collect anyone's tooth before. The fairy stood on the window-sill outside my bedroom and muttered to herself.

"Ten Blanford Road . . . ten . . . yes."

The fairy took out a small book. I could just read the title – *Ten Tasks of the Tooth Fairy.*

The tiny creature began reading through some instructions. She had a very high-pitched voice which I could hear quite clearly through the window.

"*First locate the home of the person who has lost his or her tooth.*" The fairy left the windowsill and flew down to check our house number.

In a moment she reappeared
on the window sill. "Yes, ten."

She looked at her
book again.

"*Rule Two –
Enter the said
property*. Right."
The fairy shut
her eyes, squared
her shoulders and
walked straight at the
window. The bang
of her head on
the glass echoed
through my
whole bedroom.

Ow!

"Ow!" she said, so loudly that I was sure Mother would come in at any moment. She shook her head and took her book out again. "*Enter the said property . . . using Tooth Fairy Technique.*
Ah, tooth fairy technique.
How could I have forgotten?

I must remember to read on properly."

She began to mutter a little poem:

"Tooth Fairy, Tooth Fairy

Be soft and not scary

Enter the house

Quiet as a mouse

Shimmer, now shimmer

Enter with a glimmer."

The tiny creature began to vibrate until she was just a shimmering light, which quietly passed through the window pane and into my room.

Chapter Three

Once she was through the window, the fairy collapsed onto the end of my bed puffing noisily.

"Sssh!" I said, "You'll wake Mother."

"Oh, no, no, no, no," exclaimed the fairy crossly.

"Grown-ups never wake up when the tooth fairy comes. Why, how do you think we would get any work done if . . . ?" The fairy stopped for a moment and looked very annoyed.

"You're not supposed to be awake either. That spoils the whole thing. At least I think it does." She frowned and began thumbing through her book again.

I could see a large sign with a
"T" on it pinned to her back.

"What's the 'T' for?" I asked.

"Hmmm?" The fairy was busy
reading.

She looked up for a minute.
"Oh, that, yes, it means
'Trainee'. I'm new, you see. I've
not done a human tooth before.

I've been doing cats and dogs for
a while. I was quite good apart
from trying to
take a canine
from a Great
Dane who
wasn't ready
yet. You're
my first
actual child. Now sssh!"

Give me
that
tooth
NOW!

She went back to her book.
"Yes, here it is. *Rule Number
Three – Check the child is asleep.*"
The fairy snapped her book shut
with a sigh. "Well, you're not
asleep, are you? I suppose I shall

have to come back tomorrow."

The fairy got up, shook herself and moved towards the window. She looked miserable.

"Don't go!" I called. "I tell you what, I could pretend to be asleep. No-one would know."

"Really?" said the fairy, stopping on the window sill and having a think. "That would be awfully kind."

"No trouble at all." I shut my eyes and waited for her to get on with taking the tooth.

I could hear her muttering to herself.

"Better be quick. Don't want to get caught. What's the next thing?" She was obviously in a hurry because I don't think she checked her book properly.

"Rule Four . . . can't remember. Never mind. Rule Five. What is Rule Five? Oh yes – take the child," she murmured and before I knew it something very odd started to happen.

The fairy chanted:

"Now fly, fly
High in the sky
The time is at hand
For Tooth Fairy Land"

Slowly I began to rise above
my bed. I knew I wasn't sleeping
because I could see my teddy
bear on the bed below me.

I could feel myself getting
smaller until I was just as tiny
as my fairy friend. I don't know
how I stayed in the air. The fairy
wasn't holding me.

We floated twice around
the bedroom and then with a
shimmer and a shivery feeling we
flew out of the room. We went
straight through the window
pane as if it wasn't there.

We floated over the front garden, over the gravel path to the gate, across the night sky and away.

Chapter Four

If you've never flown through the
night sky in just your pyjamas,
you will never know how thrilling

it was. It was wonderful.
We flew over my
school and the playing
fields. We flew over
the milkman who
was just starting work.
We flew over a pub where the
landlord was asleep on the sofa.

We flew over a house which
was having a
noisy party. We
flew on and on
towards the stars.
I felt quite safe
and very relaxed
and even though I was high
above the ground. After a while
we flew into a
large cloud and
very gently
we descended
through the
mist to the
ground.

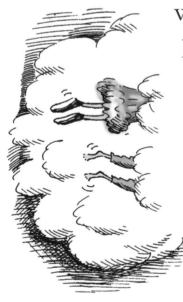

It took a moment for the mist
to clear. We appeared to have
arrived in a strange new land.
A land that was very white and
very odd.

At first I couldn't make out
what anything was but the
fairy seemed quite at home.

"This way," she called,
hurrying on ahead of me.

I followed her even though
I was beginning to feel a little
anxious.

After a moment I saw a huge
valley below me like a deep
black hole. It was dark and scary
with lots of broken bits of white
littering the steep sides.

"That's the Valley of No Repair," said the fairy, stopping to look me straight in the eye. "It's full of teeth which haven't been looked after."

A bridge appeared before us. It was pure white and surprisingly strong when you stepped onto it.

Valley of No Repair

WELCOME TO REAL TOOTH LAND
read the signs as we crossed over
to the other side of the valley.

It was an amazing place.
Everything was made of teeth.
Hundreds of fairies were going
about their business.

Lots of them were carrying teeth or swapping teeth for money at the bank.

We hadn't gone very far when suddenly there was a terrible noise.

"Trainee Twelve!" boomed an incredibly loud voice. Everyone went silent.

Nothing could be heard except a couple of teeth chattering in someone's arms.

My fairy stopped in her tracks.

"Oh dear, it's the Head Fairy," she said.

A huge fairy, dripping with
bits of gold and silver filling,
stood in front of us.

Four guards stood to attention behind her.

My trainee looked quite frightened. The giant reached out and grabbed my shoulder.

"What, may I ask, is this?" demanded the fairy.

"Ah," said my trainee. "It's the child I went to collect . . ."

"Not the child!" screamed the Head Fairy. "The tooth. You're supposed to collect the tooth."

My trainee grabbed her rule book and began to thumb through it. "But it says – *Rule Five – Take the child . . .'s tooth.* Ah . . ." The little fairy blushed.

"I'm so sorry. I . . . uh . . .
forgot to read on."

Everyone was watching as
the huge fairy leant forward
and whispered urgently to the
trainee.

"Children are not allowed
here. What have you done?
Now we'll have to get rid of it.
Guards, arrest them both."

Chapter Five

We were both taken to a large room where a lot of fairies had gathered. Everyone seemed most upset. The Head Fairy was ranting, "This is outrageous. Nothing like this has happened since gob-stoppers were invented."

"Oh dear," said my trainee fairy, miserably. She stood in a corner with drooping wings and her head hung low.

Behind a very high desk sat a white-haired old fairy. The guards stood to attention as he spoke.

"Trainee Twelve, you are charged with bringing a child to Tooth Fairy Land, where no child should ever enter. First witness." The old fairy banged a toothbrush on the desk and the guards pushed me forward.

A fairy in a black cloak held out a small mirror in front of my face.

"Say aaah!" said the fairy in a bored voice.

"Aaah," I said obediently.

The fairy handed me a cup of pink water.

"Rinse and spit."

I took a sip of the water and spat it out in a bucket by  my side. "You may proceed," said the old fairy.

"Tell us what happened."

"Well," I said. "I was in bed and then . . ."

The old fairy banged his
brush on the desk again and
announced, "Just as I thought.
Disgraceful. Trainee Twelve, you
will be stripped of your wings
and never collect another
tooth again.

Right, time for tea."
The guards
grabbed my
weeping
trainee and
everyone
started to leave.

"Wait!" I cried. "What about me?"

There was a silence as the old fairy looked at me. "You, child?" he said.

"I have to go home." He shook his head.

Wait !

"You can't leave. Tooth Fairy
Land is supposed to be secret
and now that you've been, you
will tell everyone.

"This is very serious."

"Very serious," muttered all the
fairies in the court, shaking their
heads.

"Look, it wasn't my fault or the trainee's either. She just wasn't ready for the job." The entire room was silent as I carried on.

"If my mother finds me missing in the morning she will cause a terrible fuss. What if the word got out that one of your tooth fairies made a mistake?

That you had taken a child
instead of a tooth? Why, no
child in the world would ever
trust you with their teeth again.
There would be no more new
teeth in Tooth Fairy Land."

A gasp ran through the fairies.

"Tooth Fairy Land would begin to decay and you could never get another tooth to repair it."

The old fairy looked worried.
"She's right. What can we
do?"

I was rather nervous but I
stood my ground and looked
at them all. "You must agree

never again to send trainees
out alone. I think they need
someone to help them. If you
don't agree then I shall have to
tell all the children that it isn't
safe to put their
teeth under
the pillow."

There
was a
dreadful
silence and
I thought
perhaps I had gone too far.
The toothbrush banged once
more and the old fairy spoke.

"I'm ready to announce my verdict. The child is right.

Collecting teeth is a serious business and we should not have sent a young trainee to do a proper fairy's job. In future all trainees will be accompanied by a qualified fairy until they are ready to take on full teeth-collecting responsibility. Trainee Twelve – you are forgiven but will undergo rigorous re-training."

"And me?" I said. "Yes, you may go home but you must promise to tell no-one about this."

"Not ever?"

There was some discussion until the old fairy said, "We realize that it would be a difficult secret to keep for ever so we have decided – you must stay silent until we have had time to ensure such a disaster never happens again. You may not reveal this 'adventure' for many years. You must wait till you have a grandchild who loses a tooth. If you agree, then you may go home."

I nodded.

All the fairies gathered to see me off. The Head Fairy herself walked with me and my trainee to the bridge over the Valley of No Repair.

Soon the three of us were across the valley and back into the mists. Once again we floated high above the ground. Before I knew it, I was back to normal size and in my bed. The Head Fairy winked at me as she took my tooth and laid a brand new shiny penny in its place . . .

Chapter Six

Granny sighed and finished her champagne. "Thank goodness it all turned out well or I wouldn't be here telling the story."

Jessica looked at her granny who was smiling. "Is that true, Granny?"

Granny grinned. "Things are sometimes true if you believe them." She got up from her chair.

"Let me know whether or not
you get a pound for your tooth."
Jessica went home with the
tooth and put it under her pillow.

That night, while Jessica slept,
when the hall clock chimed four
in the morning, there were not

one but two tiny shadows
standing shimmering at her
bedroom window.

THE END

Colour First Readers

Welcome to Colour First Readers. The following
pages are intended for any adults (parents, relatives,
teachers) who may buy these books to share the
stories with youngsters. The pages explain a little
about the different stages of learning to read and
offer some suggestions about how best to support
children at a very important point in their reading
development.

Children start to learn about reading as soon as
someone reads a book aloud to them when they are
babies. Book-loving babies grow into toddlers who
enjoy sitting on a lap listening to a story, looking
at pictures or joining in with familiar words. Young
children who have listened to stories start school with
an expectation of enjoyment from books and this
positive outlook helps as they are taught to read in
the more formal context of school.

Cracking the code

Before they can enjoy reading for and to themselves,
all children have to learn how to crack the alphabetic
code and make meaning out of the lines and
squiggles we call letters and punctuation. Some
lucky pupils find the process of learning to read
undemanding; some find it very hard.

Most children, within two or three years, become confident at working out what is written on the page. During this time they will probably read collections of books which are graded; that is, the books introduce a few new words and increase in length, thus helping youngsters gradually to build up their growing ability to work out the words and understand basic meanings.

Eventually, children will reach a crucial point when, without any extra help, they can decode words in an entire book, albeit a short one. They then enter the next phase of becoming a reader.

Making meaning

It is essential, at this point, that children stop seeing progress as gradually 'climbing a ladder' of books of ever-increasing difficulty. There is a transition stage between building word recognition skills and enjoying reading a story. Up until now, success has depended on getting the words right but to get pleasure from reading to themselves, children need to fully comprehend the content of what they read. Comprehension will only be reached if focus is put on understanding meaning and that can only happen if the reader is not hesitant when decoding. At this fragile, transition stage, decoding should be so easy that it slowly becomes automatic. Reading a book with ease enables children to get lost in the story, to enjoy the unfolding narrative at the same time as perfecting their newly learned word recognition skills.

At this stage in their reading development, children need to:

- Practice their newly established early decoding skills at a level which eventually enables them to do it automatically

- Concentrate on making sensible meanings from the words they decode

- Develop their ability to understand when meanings are 'between the lines' and other use of literary language

- Be introduced, very gradually, to longer books in order to build up stamina as readers

In other words, new readers need books that are well within their reading ability and that offer easy encounters with humour, inference, plot-twists etc. In the past, there have been very few children's books that provided children with these vital experiences at an early stage. Indeed, some children had to leap from highly controlled teaching materials to junior novels.

This experience often led to reluctance in youngsters who were not yet confident enough to tackle longer books.

Matching the books to reading development

Colour First Readers fill the gap between early reading and children's literature and, in doing so, support inexperienced readers at a vital time in their reading development. Reading aloud to children continues to be very important even after children have learned to read and, as they are well written by popular children's authors, Colour First Readers are great to read aloud. The stories provide plenty of opportunities for adults to demonstrate different voices or expression and, in a short time, give lots to talk about and enjoy together.

Each book in the series combines a number of highly beneficial features, including:

- Well-written and enjoyable stories by popular children's authors

- Unthreatening amounts of print on a page

- Unrestricted but accessible vocabularies

- A wide interest age to suit the different ages at which children might reach the transition stage of reading development

- Different sorts of stories – traditional, set in the past, present or future, real life and fantasy, comic and serious, adventures, mysteries etc.

- A range of engaging illustrations by different illustrators

- Stories which are as good to read aloud to children as they are to be read alone

All in all, Colour First Readers are to be welcomed for children throughout the early primary school years – not only for learning to read but also as a series of good stories to be shared by everyone. I like to think that the word 'Readers' in the title of this series refers to the many young children who will enjoy these books on their journey to becoming lifelong bookworms.

Prue Goodwin
Honorary Fellow of the University of Reading

Helping children to enjoy *The Troublesome Tooth Fairy*

If a child can read a page or two fluently, without struggling with the words at all, then he/she should be able to read this book alone. However, children are all different and need different levels of support to help them become confident enough to read a book to themselves.

Some young readers will not need any help to get going; they can just get on with enjoying the story. Others may lack confidence and need help getting into the story. For these children, it may help if you talk about what might happen in the book.

Explore the title, cover and first few illustrations with them, making comments and suggestions about any clues to what might happen in the story. Read the first chapter aloud together. Don't make it a chore. If they are still reluctant to do it alone, read the whole book with them, making it an enjoyable experience.

The following suggestions will not be necessary every time a book is read but, every so often, when a story has been particularly enjoyed, children love responding to it through creative activities.

Before reading

Children are usually ready to read Colour First
Readers around the age of six which coincides
with the time when milk-teeth are falling out. This
means that, at this stage in their life, *The Troublesome
Tooth Fairy* is an ideal book to read. Just in case any
children are unfamiliar with the job of the Tooth
Fairy, remind them about the importance of leaving
teeth under the pillow.

During reading

Asking questions about a story can be really helpful
to support understanding but don't ask too many –
and don't make it feel like test on what has happened.
Relate the questions to the child's own experiences
and imagination. For example, ask: 'How much
money does the Tooth Fairy leave for your teeth?' or
'Would you like to visit Tooth Fairy Land?'

Responding to the book

If your child has enjoyed this story, it increases the fun
by doing something creative in response. If possible,
provide art materials and dressing up clothes so that
they can make things, play at being characters, write
and draw, act out a scene or respond in some other
way to the story.

Activities for children

If you have enjoyed reading this story, you could:

- Look back at the first few pages. Jessica goes to show her granny the gap in her smile where a tooth has just come out. Read about what granny looks like and draw a picture of her. The rest of the book is Jessica's granny telling a story about what happened when she was a little girl.

- Open your mouth wide and look in the mirror at your own teeth. Can you see:

    • front teeth called incisors which help us bite into food?

    • teeth at the back called molars which are for chewing and grinding food?

    • any gaps where a tooth has come out?

- Look at Chapter 2 to see what Granny said about the tooth fairy who came to her bedroom. Find the words to fill the spaces in these sentences:

    1. This was a _____ tooth fairy.
    A troublesome, t_____ tooth fairy .

    2. She was about _____ centimetres tall and dressed in _____ and _____ .

3. She had never been to _____ **anyone's**
   _____ **before.**

4. The fairy stood on the _____ **outside**
   my _____ **.**

- Write or draw something about the trip to 'Tooth Fairy Land'. What do they see? Who do they meet? What happens to the trainee tooth fairy?

- Get a pencil, some paper and some colours to make a poster about keeping your teeth healthy. You can include something about cleaning your teeth and about visiting the dentist regularly. If teeth are not kept clean they may end up in the Valley of No Repair.

ALSO AVAILABLE AS COLOUR FIRST READERS